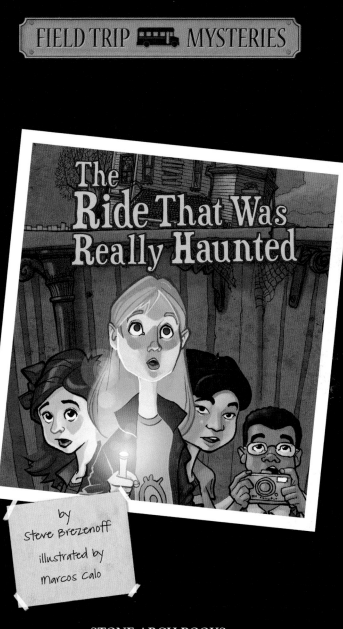
The
Ride That Was
Really Haunted

by
Steve Brezenoff

illustrated by
Marcos Calo

STONE ARCH BOOKS
a capstone imprint

r Samantha Archer,

Field Trip Mysteries are published by Stone Arch Books
A Capstone Imprint
1710 Roe Crest Drive
North Mankato, Minnesota 56003
www.capstonepub.com

Library of Congress Cataloging-in-Publication Data
Brezenoff, Steven.
    The ride that was really haunted / by Steve Brezenoff ; illustrated by Marcos Calo.
        p. cm. -- (Field trip mysteries)
    Summary:
    ISBN-13: 978-1-4342-3224-3 (library binding)
    ISBN-13: 978-1-4342-3427-8 (pbk.)
    ISBN-13: 978-1-4342-4166-5 (pbk.)

    1. Amusement parks--Juvenile fiction. 2. Haunted houses--Juvenile fiction. 3. School field trips--Juvenile fiction. 4. Detective and mystery stories. [1. Mystery and detective stories. 2. Amusement parks--Fiction. 3. Haunted houses--Fiction. 4. School field trips--Fiction.] I. Calo, Marcos, ill. II. Title. III. Series: Brezenoff, Steven. Field trip mysteries.
    PZ7.B7576Ri 2011
    813.6--dc22
                                                        2011002176

Art Director/Graphic Designer: Kay Fraser

Summary: The Haunted House ride at Fun City is rumored to be haunted by the ghost of someone who died there, and when Samantha "Sam" Archer and her friends get trapped inside they need to find the truth.

Printed in the United States of America in Stevens Point, Wisconsin.
052012
                    006764R

TABLE OF CONTENTS

STUDENTS

Samantha Archer

A.K.A: Sam

D.O.B: August 20th

POSITION: 6th Grade

Why are these kids so interested in field trips? I will look into this!

INTERESTS:
Old movies, field trips

KNOWN ASSOCIATES:
Duran, Catalina; Garrison, Edward; and Shoo, James.

NOTES:
Samantha frequently uses expressions many of the students—and even some of the teachers—do not understand. These seem to come from the old movies she watches at home.

Samantha recently called me Mr. Spade's "Bruno." What does this mean? I will look into this, too.

CHAPTER ONE

FUN CITY

At our school, sixth graders always look forward to our October field trip. For one thing, it's on a Saturday. That means there doesn't have to be any educational value at all! It's just for fun. And it is fun. We go to Fun City! That's the best amusement park for miles around.

Finally the day arrived. The school bus pulled up to Fun City.

"Okay, ladies and germs," Mr. Kipper said. He is our gym teacher. "Here we are. Everyone, please stay in your seats until the bus comes to a complete stop."

Of course, we were all standing up to look out the window already.

"Look at that, Sam!" Gum shouted, grabbing my wrist. "The Terrible Twister. It's the biggest roller coaster in the state."

"That's where we're going first," I said. I love rides. The scarier the better.

"Um, I'll meet you two at the exit," Cat said.

I smiled. Cat is pretty brave most of the time, but when it comes to rides, she prefers slow stuff.

"And I'll stay on the ground to get good photos of you two," Egg said. He tapped the camera hanging around his neck.

He always has his camera. It sure comes in handy when we're solving another mystery. Somehow, the four of us always end up with a crime to solve.

"Good thinking," Gum said. "I can't wait to see the goofy faces Sam makes when the ride goes upside down on the second turn."

"Oh, please," I said. "You're the one who's going to spit out his gum."

The bus's brakes squeaked and hissed. The driver swung the door open. "Step off carefully, please," he said.

"You heard the man," Mr. Kipper said. "Everyone off, and be careful. That means no running."

Anton Gutman knocked my shoulder as I got up. "Watch it," he said as he pushed past. "I'm walking here."

He wasn't walking, though. He was running. Pushing past everyone. He got to the front of the bus first. One of his goon friends was right behind him.

"Anton better not ruin this trip," Gum said. "He's always making trouble."

"Gum, my friend," I said. I threw an arm around his shoulders. "If the worst trouble we have today is Anton Gutman, it'll be our easiest field trip ever."

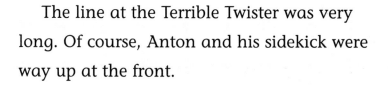
The line at the Terrible Twister was very long. Of course, Anton and his sidekick were way up at the front.

Egg, Cat, Gum, and I got in line at the back. A little sign right where we stood read, "From this point in line, the wait will be about 3 hours."

"Three hours?" Gum said.

"Well, let's do a different ride first," Cat suggested. "Maybe something a little . . . slower?"

"And closer to the ground," Egg added.

"Okay," I said. "Let's check back later, after lunch."

As we stepped off the line, a man in a long coat knocked into me. "Oh, pardon me," I said.

He spun and faced me. His face was old and dry, and his eyes looked sad. "Watch your step from now on," the man said. "The park is a dangerous place."

"Um, sorry," I said.

Then he hurried off. I watched as he disappeared behind a snack stand.

"That was weird," Gum said. "I wonder who that guy was. He sure didn't seem like the type of person who wanted to hang around at Fun City."

Egg held up his camera. "Nope," he said. On the display was a clear photo of the man I'd bumped. "I think this guy looks like an escaped convict," Egg added.

"Oh, Egg," Cat said. "He was just a little odd. I don't think that makes him a criminal."

"I bet he's security," I said, tapping my chin. "He's undercover security."

Gum shook his head. "I'm with Egg on this one," he said. "Convict."

The four of us headed down the main sidewalk looking for a ride we could all agree on.

"How about this?" Gum asked. He pointed.

We were stopped in front of a creepy old building. It looked like an old three-story house. The windows were busted, and the porch buckled and creaked. From inside the building, we could hear creepy wailing and moaning.

"The haunted house?" I said. "I don't know. What do you say, Cat?" I knew Cat could be scared of things sometimes. I didn't want her to be freaked out.

Cat shrugged as we watched a car full of kids come out of the exit. "Looks pretty slow," she said. "I don't mind scary, as long as it's not fast."

"Looks good to me," Egg said.

The four of us strode up to the ticket collector. She was facing away from us, chatting into her cell phone.

"Excuse us," Cat said.

Without turning around, the young woman put up her finger to silence us. She went on yapping into her phone.

"Listen," she said. She seemed angry. "Just because I'm on the schedule to work through lunch doesn't mean I have to. If I want a lunch break, I'll take one," she snapped. "Who cares? No one's interested in this dumb haunted house anyway." She laughed.

"It's the **lamest** ride ever."

"Hello?" Gum said. She ignored us.

"Miss?" Egg tried. Still, she ignored us.

"Give me a ticket each, you guys," I said. Gum, Egg, and Cat each handed me one ride ticket. I took one of mine and left the four tickets on the counter.

"When she's done chatting, she can take our tickets," I said. "Now let's go."

The others weren't sure at first. But when I hit the start button on the pole next to the ticket booth and jumped into the car as it slowly rolled toward the entrance, they had no choice.

"You're crazy!" Cat said. But she and the boys jogged after me and climbed aboard.

The car slowly picked up speed and headed right for the house. In front of us was a dirty old wall, covered in spider webs and "DO NOT ENTER" signs.

"Wow," Egg said. He took a few photos. "It looks like a real haunted house."

"I heard it *is* real," Cat said in hushed tones. As she spoke, our shadows flickered on the wall, cast only by old lamps hanging above us.

I chuckled. "Oh, come on," I said. "Not another ghost story."

Cat nodded. Her face went serious. "It's true," she said. "I told my mom about the trip, and she told me about something that happened twenty years ago."

"What happened?" Gum asked.

"A bunch of riders got locked inside the haunted house," Cat said. "Somebody got hurt. Mom wouldn't say if someone had died, but I think someone did. No one knows why they were trapped there."

"So where's the ghost come into it?" Egg asked. He took a photo of Cat as she went on.

"They say he's been haunting the ride ever since," she said.

"Why?" I asked.

Cat shrugged. "To make sure other people suffer the same fate?" she suggested.

"Well, anyway," I said. "The ride's about to get going, I think. Look."

I pointed up ahead. Our car was heading for the big staircase up to the second floor. At the top, a suit of armor waited for us.

"That thing will probably come to life when we get close," I said. "Watch."

Our car reached the stairs with a great clank. Slowly, we climbed. As we got close, the suit of armor began to move.

"Told you," I said.

The suit threw up its arms and gave a loud shout. Suddenly it grabbed its sword and swung it at us. Gum screamed and ducked.

In front of us, ghosts and witches slid out of doorways, cackling and crying out. It might have been scary at some point, but the machines were all so old and beaten up, they wouldn't have scared my baby cousin.

"This is lame," I said.

Just then, two figures appeared from a door at the end of the tunnel. They were hunched over and moving toward us.

"Those don't look fake," Cat said.

Egg raised his camera and snapped some pictures. "They must be," he said.

"Of course they are," Gum said. "I'm not afraid."

They came closer and closer, faster and faster. Their voices sounded so real.

"They must be actors in costumes," I said. "It's nothing to be afraid of."

Suddenly they were upon us. They shouted and screamed and grabbed at Egg's shirt.

"They're not actors!" Cat shouted. She shrieked and batted at their arms.

"Let's get out of here!" Gum screamed.

The monsters got right into the car with us. I tried to climb out from under the guard bar across my lap, but it was locked.

I looked up.
One of the monsters
was leaning toward me,
his hands out to grab
my throat.

"Get off me!" I cried out. I batted at its hands, and the monster backed up.

"Ow," it said.

Cat pulled back and slapped the other monster across the face. "Hey!" it said. "No hitting."

Then both monsters climbed off the car and ran down the tracks toward the suit of armor.

"Quick, Egg," I said, "take a photo — and don't forget the flash."

Egg snapped a bunch of pictures. The flash distracted the pair of monsters, and they ran right into the suit of armor. It fell off its stand with a loud *clank*.

"Let's see those photos," I said. Egg leaned over to me and showed me the display on his camera. "Just as I thought," I said.

The others leaned over to look, too.

"Anton!" Gum said. "I knew it."

"Yeah right," I said. "You were scared."

"Was not," Gum said quietly.

The car was still moving down the hall.

"The problem is, now he's gotten away,"
I said. "I wish we could have held him until
Mr. Kipper was around."

"Yeah," Cat said. "He and his friend ought
to get in trouble for that gag. Not cool."

"They could have really hurt us," Egg said.

"Or themselves," I added.

"The exit's this way," Cat told us. "So we'll
have to come across them again before they
get out, right?"

"I guess so," I said. The car crept down
the hall into a big ballroom. The sound of
thunder crashed through the speakers, and
lightning flashed in the big windows.

Then, suddenly, the car stopped and the lap bars opened.

"Um," Gum said. "Is this the end?"

I climbed out of the car and got down on my knees in front of it. "Nope," I said. "The tracks keep going."

"So, why did the car stop?" Cat asked.

Footsteps echoed from the hall behind us. "Someone's coming," I said.

"Probably Anton and his friend," Gum said. "Let's hide and grab them when they come in."

I nodded, and the four of us quietly moved toward the door. Cat and I stood on one side. Egg and Gum stood on the other.

I held my breath and waited. The footsteps grew louder and closer.

"Now!" I shouted. The four of us dove at the doorway and knocked the two boys to the ground.

"Now we've got you," I said. "Mr. Kipper will put you in detention until graduation."

Anton wriggled and struggled. "Let me go!" he shouted.

"Yeah," said the other boy. It was Anton's friend Peter. "Get off us."

Gum sat across his chest. The kid couldn't budge. "Should we let them go?" Gum asked.

"I suppose," I said. "Let's put them in the car. Once the ride gets moving they'll be stuck with us, and we can turn them in later."

Gum nodded and stood up. Peter stood up too. "No way," he said. "I'll find another way out." And he ran off down the hall again, into the darkness.

Anton made a break for it too, but I grabbed his arm. "Oh, no you don't," I said. "And don't worry. Your friend will be back."

"Darn it," Anton said, slumping over. The four of us dragged him to the car, but when we got there, something wasn't right.

"Hey, does something seem different to you guys?" I asked.

The others looked around.

"It's awfully quiet," Cat said.

Gum nodded slowly. "Too quiet."

"You morons," Anton said. "The ride is off. Of course it's quiet."

"Off?" Egg repeated.

"Then," Cat said in a whisper, "how will we get out?"

"You did this," Gum said. I don't think I've ever seen him so mad. His face started to turn red as he grabbed Anton's shirt collar. "You'd better fix it, buddy."

Anton smiled. "I have no idea what you're talking about," he said.

"You do too," Cat said. "First you put on some goofy monster costumes and tried to scare us."

"And now you've trapped us all in here," I said.

"This is dangerous business, buster," I said.

"Oh, listen to yourself," Anton said. He paced around, laughing and shaking his head. "Do you think I'd lock myself in here? On purpose? With you dorks?!"

I thought it over. "Maybe not," I said. "Maybe Peter did this."

"Why would he?" Anton asked.

"To be a jerk," Cat muttered.

Egg nodded. "Good point, Cat," he said. "That sounds exactly like the kind of thing one of you would do."

Anton rolled his eyes. "I promise, it wasn't us," he said. "All we did was see you dorks getting on the ride. We bought two monster masks and ran in when your car entered, then hid upstairs to scare you."

"The lady at the front just let you walk in?" I asked.

"With no car?" Gum added. "And no ticket?"

Anton waved us off. "That lady wasn't paying any attention," he said. "She probably doesn't even know the ride is stopped."

I chewed my cheek. "That's true," I said. "She was in La La Land when we saw her, talking on the phone. We'll have to figure out how to get out of here ourselves."

"I don't think this is a great idea," Anton said.

He was next to me, up in front of the pack. I had my penlight out, and I shined it at the ground so we could follow the tracks.

"Why not?" I asked. "If we follow the tracks, they're bound to lead to an exit."

"Trust us, Anton," Gum said. He blew a bubble. When it popped, Anton jumped. "We know what we're doing," Gum went on. "We figure stuff out on every trip."

Cat laughed. "Yeah," she said. "When we get back to the bus, we'll help Mr. Kipper figure out what a brat you've been."

"Oh, please," Anton said. "Mr. Kipper will never believe you four over me."

"Why not?" Egg asked.

"I'm his favorite student, that's why," Anton said. "And he doesn't like you."

"He does too!" Cat said.

Anton smiled. "Nope," he said. "He doesn't like you because you don't like sports. Even you, Sam. He wants you to take sports seriously and join the softball team, but you're too big of a dork to join the team, I guess."

I didn't have a comeback for that. We all knew Mr. Kipper didn't like anyone who didn't love gym class.

But I knew I had it worse than the others. I was always good at sports, but I never cared. That's what bothered Mr. Kipper the most.

"Uh-oh," Egg said. "Now what?"

I looked down.

The track split in two directions. We had to make a decision.

"I guess we should flip a coin," I said.

"What?" Anton said. "You're going to leave our fate to a coin toss?! You're insane, all of you."

We ignored him. Cat pulled a lucky penny from her pocket and flipped it.

"Heads, we go right," I said as it flipped through the air.

It landed on the floor with a clink, then rolled away.

"Where'd it go?" Egg said.

I shined the light across the floor and caught a glimpse of the penny rolling away. "There it is," I said. I jogged after it. "I'll check what lands up."

I ran across the floor after the penny as it hit the far wall. I stood over it with my penlight, waiting for the coin to finish spinning and pick a side. Finally it did, and I bent down to pick it up.

"Heads," I called to the others. Then I raised my penlight and pointed it toward the group. "That means we go —"

But then someone stepped between me and my friends, blocking my light.

"Is that you, Peter?" I asked, squinting into the darkness.

"Get out of here!" a raspy voice shouted back. The figure lunged toward me. "The haunted house is a dangerous place!"

Someone grabbed my arm. Cat's face was close to mine. "We have to get out of this room," she said. "It's the ghost!"

CHAPTER SEVEN

GUARDED BY GHOSTS

I let Cat pull me away and we joined the others as they ran along the dark tracks.

"That wasn't the ghost," I said between breaths. "It was that security guard."

"What?" Gum said.

"The undercover one from the roller-coaster line," I said.

The four of us tumbled through the darkness until we reached a door. Egg threw it open and we all went in.

"Where are we?" Cat asked.

"Hold on," Gum said. I heard him fumbling in the dark, and soon the room lit up. "There."

We were in a small room. There was a table in the center, and several metal boxes along the walls that held lots of switches and knobs.

"Must be the control room," Egg said. "We can probably control the whole haunted house from here."

"Good," I said. "Let's find the "on" switch and get out of here."

Gum was a step ahead of me. "That might be a problem," he said.

He was holding two thick cables, both frayed at the end like they'd been cut.

"Someone cut the main cable," I said. "I guess we'll have to walk out after all."

"Hey," Cat said. "You guys."

We turned to Cat. She stood by the door with her arms out.

"What, Cat?" I said.

"It's Anton," she said. "He's gone."

We left the control room and followed the tracks back to the split. "I guess this time we'll try the other tracks," I said.

"I just hope we don't run into that ghost again," Cat said.

"It wasn't a ghost," I said. "It was that guy we saw near the Terrible Twister."

"You mean the guy you thought was a security guard?" Gum asked.

I nodded.

"I'm not so sure about that anymore, though," I said. "In fact, I think half of the ghost story is sort of true."

The others stopped short. "Wait, what?" Gum said.

"Yeah," Egg said. "Are you telling us you believe a ghost story?"

"Sam, the great detective," Cat said, "believes a ghost story?"

"Let's just say I believe the non-ghost part," I explained. "I believe something happened here — something tragic — twenty years ago. And I believe the man responsible is here again."

"Like, to celebrate the anniversary?" Gum said.

"Or to repeat it," I said. "Here are the tracks. Let's go left this time."

We walked for a while. At every turn I expected to run into someone: maybe Peter, maybe Anton, maybe the creepy guy. That last one was the scariest possibility, I admit.

"Hey, Sam," Egg said. "Shine your light up here."

I found Egg in the darkness and stepped up next to him to see where he was pointing. I followed his finger with my penlight and found a dusty old sign: Emergency Exit.

"There we go," Gum said. "Good eyes, Egg."

I pushed on the handle, but it wouldn't budge. "It's locked," I said. "Or maybe it's stuck."

"It probably hasn't been used in twenty years," Cat pointed out. "That was the last time anyone got stuck in here like this, remember?"

I nodded. "Let's try together," I said. The four of us leaned on the door. "One, two, three! Push!"

We shoved with all our might. The door creaked and its hinges squeaked.

"Almost there," I said with a grunt. "Keep pushing!"

The door slowly moved. It shrieked against the floor as it swung open.

I expected sunlight to show through the crack as we pushed, but only darkness waited once the door was fully open.

"Another hallway," Gum said. "Great."

"Look there," Cat said. She pointed down the long hallway at a light glowing at the end. "An exit sign."

"Let's go," Egg said. The four of us ran down the hall. The sign pointed to the right. Down that hall, we saw sunlight sneaking in cracks around a door way at the end. To the left was more deep darkness.

"This way," Gum said. He turned right and headed down the hall.

I turned to follow, with Egg and Cat, and a door slammed behind me.

"What was that?" I asked. The others stopped.

"It was nothing," Gum said. "It was probably the door we just opened, closing on its own."

"Yeah, Sam," Cat said, smiling. "We're almost out. Let's keep moving."

"That door?" Egg said. "Close on its own? No way."

"Egg's right," I said. "That door would take a big push from a few people to close again."

"So, what are you saying?" Gum said.

"I'm saying that was a different door," I said. "And it was probably slammed by the culprit in this haunted-house sabotage."

"Or Anton or Peter," Cat said.

I shrugged. "Or them," I said. "But it might be the guy behind this whole thing. And we can't let him get away."

Gum and Cat looked at each other, then at me and Egg. Gum sighed. "We're not leaving yet, are we?" he asked.

I shook my head.

"We're going the other way," Cat said, "to catch the creepy guy. Aren't we?"

Egg nodded.

"All right," Gum said. "Let's do this."

"It's got to be Peter and Anton," Gum hissed in the darkness.

The four of us walked slowly down the long hallway. The battery in my penlight had died, so I kept a hand on the wall beside me. Egg and Gum were in front, so Egg could sometimes take a photo. That would light up the hallway with the flash. So far, it was working okay.

"Who else are our suspects?" I asked.

"Mr. Kipper," Cat said.

"To him, we're the dorks who hate sports," Egg said.

I laughed. "Hey, we're not dorks," I said. "And he's always asking me to join track."

Cat shrugged. "Maybe he's sick of you saying no," she said. "Maybe he's so sick of us four that he'd lock us in the haunted house."

I shook my head. "Who else?" I asked.

"The weird guy," Egg said.

"Yeah. And remember the woman working at the ticket booth?" I asked. "She sure didn't seem happy to be here."

"True," Egg said. "But what motive would she have for sabotaging the ride?"

"Maybe she didn't sabotage it," I began.

Then Egg cut me off. "Shhh," he said. "Everyone stop. Do you hear that?"

We all stopped. I strained to listen. It was completely quiet. But when we started walking again, I heard it too. "There," I said. "Footsteps."

"It's just an echo," Gum said. "We've been in here so long, we're going crazy. I bet Anton, Peter, and even the creepy guy are long gone by now."

"It's no echo," I said in a whisper. "Someone's in the darkness, watching us."

Then the footsteps were faster. Whoever it was had heard me, and now he was running away.

"Follow him!" I said. I took off running.

My friends were close behind me. Before we knew it, we were back inside the "haunted" part of the building. "Watch your step," I said.

Then I stepped on something. A witch popped out from the wall and blocked our path.

Egg screamed and Cat fell to the ground. The witch stood over us, cackling and shaking.

Gum helped Cat to her feet. "Are you okay?" he asked. Cat nodded.

"How did whoever we're chasing avoid that witch?" I asked.

"They'd have to know this place really well," Egg said.

"Then it's not Anton or Peter," Cat said.

"You know who would know this place?" I asked.

"The ghost!" Cat said.

I nodded. "Exactly," I said.

"So now what do we do?" Gum said.

We were hopelessly lost, deep inside the haunted house. The footsteps were gone, my penlight was history, and we were all hungry for lunch.

"I think I can find the way back to the control room," Egg said. "I've been snapping a lot of pictures. I can put together a pretty good map."

"Cool," Gum said.

"Good thinking," I said. "Let's head there. There might be a phone we missed."

"Or a light switch," Cat added. "That would help."

Egg shuffled through his pictures. By looking at his pictures, and the order he'd taken them, he could tell when and where to turn.

As we walked through the ride, he told us what to do and where to go. We were back at the control room in no time.

"Nice going, Egg," Cat said.

I looked around the room and said, "Let's see if we can shed some light on this case."

"Here," Gum said. He flicked a switch on the wall, and the light overhead came on.

"Well, it's a start," I said.

Then I spotted the big cable. Before, it had been cut in two. Now it was fine.

"Look," I said. "Someone patched the main cable."

"Who could have done that?" Egg asked.

"Not Anton or Peter," Gum said. "Those two troublemakers wouldn't do anything to help anyone else."

"Maybe to help themselves, though," I said. "Hmm."

"Sam, you've got to come over and look at this," Cat said, looking at something on the wall. "It's a picture of the staff from twenty years ago."

I went over to Cat and examined what she was looking at. It was a clipping from a newspaper article.

The caption said, "Haunted House staff at the time of the accident."

I recognized one of the faces right away. "Aha," I said, smiling. "Just as I thought. There's our creepy man."

"You mean the weirdo running around in here," Gum said, "is the same guy who ran the haunted house twenty years ago?"

I smiled and was about to answer.

Then Anton came barging into the office. "There you dorks are," he said. "I spotted the light on in here and came running."

Peter was right behind him. "We've been lost in here for like four hours!" he said.

I rolled my eyes. "More like twenty minutes," I said. "But we can leave now. I've solved the mystery. Let's head to the emergency exit again. I'll explain on the way."

My friends and I headed through the door. We jogged across the ballroom, over the ride's tracks as they curved through the room. Several cars, still stopped like we left them, stood on the tracks.

We were already across the ballroom when I heard Anton in the control room, saying, "Hey, what's this switch do?"

"Don't touch it!" I said. I turned and tried to run back into the control room, but I was too late. Anton pulled a big switch. The haunted house ride shot to life.

Out in the hall, the ride's cars started rolling. Cat, Gum, Egg, and I had already crossed the tracks.

"Wait for us," Anton shouted. He and Peter ran toward us, but Anton tripped, catching his foot on the tracks.

"Help me!" he called. Peter tried to stop the haunted house, but the switch wouldn't move.

"We have to get back to the control room," I said. "Or Anton won't ever leave the haunted house!"

CHAPTER ELEVEN

SAVED

Anton was screaming and trying to pull his leg out of the track.

"We'll never make it," Egg said. He nodded toward the ride's car, barreling down the track at Anton. "The cars are coming too fast."

I took a deep breath. "Wait here," I said. Then I took off running. It was about ten yards across the big room. The cars swerved and jerked along the four sets of tracks in front of me.

As I reached the halfway point, a car darted in front of me.

"Look out, Sam!"
Gum shouted.

Without breaking my stride, I jumped.

My leg stretched out in front of me, and the other bent behind me.

When I landed on the other side, I kept right on running.

"Great jump, Sam!" Cat shouted.

"You can do it!" Egg added.

Soon another car came speeding across my path, just as I reached its tracks. Like the first time, I jumped.

I leaped clear over the moving car. This time, Egg's flash went off when I was in midair.

From there it was only a few more steps to the control room.

I jumped over Anton quickly. "Hurry!" he moaned.

I found the big switch he'd moved and turned it to "off."

The cars slowed and finally stopped.

One of them was only inches from Anton's trapped leg.

I stood over Anton and put my hands on my hips. "Next time," I said, "be more careful."

INTO THE LIGHT

"Well, this wasn't much of a haunted house," Gum said as we walked down the hallway toward the emergency exit. "But it was sure a wild ride."

"Sam," Cat said. "You were about to tell us how you solved the mystery."

"Oh, right," I said. We reached the door. "Shade your eyes," I said before pushing it open. The sunlight was blinding after being in that dark haunted house for so long.

When my eyes finally adjusted, I saw a huge crowd of people standing around the exit door. There were Mr. Kipper and the rest of the sixth graders. There were a few security guards in uniform. There was a short woman in a dark, expensive-looking suit.

And there was the man in the long coat, right in front of everyone.

"You're all okay!" Mr. Kipper said. "What a relief."

"It certainly is," said the woman in the suit. "I'm Harriet Hund, the park owner. I'm so glad you're all okay. This could've been a repeat of the accident twenty years ago."

I strode up to the man in the coat. He was the same man who caused the accident twenty years ago. "It almost was a repeat, wasn't it?" I asked.

The man nodded.

"You mean he was the one who trapped us inside?" Gum asked.

"No," I said. "But he was inside with us . . . trying to help."

"I'm afraid I didn't do a very good job," the man said.

I shrugged. "Maybe not," I said. "But we're all okay."

"Wait a second," Ms. Hund said. "I know you, don't I?" She squinted up at the man.

"I'm James," the man said. "I used to work here."

"Of course, I remember you, James," Ms. Hund said. "How have you been?" She smiled warmly at him, but James just looked down at the ground.

"I was responsible for the accident," he said. "Not today. The one twenty years ago."

Everyone gasped. "What do you mean?" Ms. Hund asked.

"I was hungry," James said. "So I left my post at the haunted house. The people must have gone in and started the ride themselves, and the machinery broke." He sighed and shook his head, looking sad. "It was a bad coincidence, but they got hurt, and it was all my fault," he said quietly. "You see, I lied and said I was there when it happened. But I wasn't."

Ms. Hund shook her head and smiled kindly at James. "That doesn't sound like your fault," she said. "That sounds like an accident. A mistake."

"And you made up for it today," I said.

"What exactly happened in there?" Ms. Hund asked.

"Well," I said, "when the ride suddenly stopped, James here did his best to make it safe for us."

"That's why he cut the wire!" Egg said. "So the cars wouldn't start up again and run us over."

"Like that one almost smushed Anton," Cat said. "But why did you tape the wire back up again?"

"I realized I'd made it nearly impossible to get out," James explained. "Without lights or any power at all, even I was having a hard time getting around. So I fixed the wire and was about to turn on the house lights when I heard you kids following me."

"Why did you run away?" I asked.

"It was foolish," James said, "but I heard you whispering. I knew you thought I was responsible. Thinking back to twenty years ago, I couldn't go through all that again. So I left. I'm sorry."

I patted his arm. "It's okay," I said. "I know who was really responsible."

"You keep saying that!" Cat said. "Why did the ride stop in the first place?"

I looked around and over the top of the crowd until I spotted a young woman walking toward the group. She was talking into her cell phone. It was the girl who had been working at the booth in front of the haunted house. "There's your answer," I said. "Ask her why the ride stopped."

Harriet's jaw dropped. "Stacy Elizabeth Hund!" she shouted. "Why did you leave your ride?"

"Uh-oh," I said quietly to my friends. "This is worse than I thought. The girl who left her post was the owner's daughter."

I watched Stacy's face as she realized what had happened. "Oh, no," she said. "Mom, I didn't know anyone was inside."

"You are in a lot of trouble, young lady," Harriet said. She marched Stacy away.

Mr. Kipper said, "I assume you four have already thanked Anton and Peter for saving you?"

"Saving us?" Gum repeated. "Please. Anton couldn't save fifty cents with a coupon."

"Yeah," Egg said. "Sam saved his life."

"Stop it," I said, trying to pull the two of them away. Anton and Peter kept their eyes on their feet.

"Are you telling me," Mr. Kipper said, "that two of my favorite athletes in the sixth grade were saved by a girl who doesn't like sports?"

"Look," Egg said. He held out his camera and clicked through to the pictures of me jumping the cars. "This is Sam." Egg clicked forward to a photo of me pulling Anton's foot out of the tracks.

"I didn't know you took that picture," Anton said.

"Me either," I said.

Mr. Kipper looked at the pictures, then at me. "Amazing," he said.

"It was nothing," I said, waving him off.

"The amazing thing, Samantha," Mr. Kipper said, "is that you're still not on my hurdles team."

"Hurdles team?" I said. "I thought you wanted me to play softball."

"Forget softball," he said. "You're a natural at hurdles. Look at this form!" He pointed at the photo of me in midair.

"Is that good?" I asked.

"It's very good," Mr. Kipper said. "It's varsity good. So, what do you say?"

"Um," I said. Gum smiled at me. Cat nodded vigorously. Egg elbowed me in the side. "Okay, I'll give it a shot."

"Wonderful!" Mr. Kipper said. Then he turned to the crowd. "Okay, everyone. Lunchtime. Let's head to the snack counter."

The whole class cheered. My friends and I hung back.

"You're really going to join the track team?" Gum asked.

"I can hardly believe it," Egg said.

"I think it's great," Cat added.

"It could be," I said. "As long as you three are there to cheer me on."

literary news

MYSTERIOUS WRITER REVEALED!

Steve Brezenoff lives in St. Paul, Minnesota, with his wife, Beth, their son, Sam, and their small, smelly dog, Harry. Besides writing books, he enjoys playing video games, riding his bicycle, and helping middle-school students work on their writing skills. Steve's ideas almost always come to him in his dreams, so he does his best writing in his pajamas.

arts & entertainment

ARTIST IS KEY TO SOLVING MYSTERY, SAY POLICE

Marcos Calo lives happily in A Coruña, Spain, with his wife, Patricia (who is also an illustrator), and their daughter, Claudia. When Marcos and Patricia aren't drawing, they like to go on long walks by the sea. They also watch a lot of films and eat Nutella sandwiches. Yum!

A Detective's Dictionary

convict (KON-vikt)–someone who has been in jail for committing a crime

culprit (KUHL-prit)–a person who is guilty of doing something wrong

dangerous (DAYN-jur-uhss)–not safe

fate (FAYT)–what will happen to a person

frayed (FRAYD)–beginning to unravel or fall apart

machinery (muh-SHEEN-uhr-ee)–the parts that make something move or work

raspy (RAS-pee)–rough-sounding, like a growl

sabotage (SAB-uh-tahj)–ruining something on purpose

suspects (SUHS-pekts)–people who may be responsible for a crime

tragic (TRAJ-ik)–very sad

undercover (uhn-dur-COV-uhr)–pretending to be someone else

Samantha Archer

Sixth Grade

A

Many people may be surprised to learn that amusement parks have been around for about five hundred years.

In the mid-sixteenth century, "pleasure gardens" were built in parts of Europe. A pleasure garden was a nice area for people to hang out in. It usually had music, fountains, flowers, bowling, and maybe a ride or two. That doesn't sound like our crazy, noisy, fast-moving amusement parks, but they did provide a fun place for a family to go.

The first roller coaster was built in France in 184⟨6⟩ The French named it the "Chemin du Centrifuge." Tha⟨t⟩ means, basically, "Gravity Way."

The first American roller coaster was built in Coney Island, in Brooklyn, New York. Introduced in 1864, and called "Switchback Gravity Pleasure Railway," it was part of a growing vacation and resort area at Coney Island.

Haunted houses have been around for centuries. In fact, there's some evidence that ancient Egyptians may have had some type of haunted houses.

Imagine what the amusement park of the future will be like!

Samantha: Well done. I'm a little afraid of roller coasters, but if people have been riding them for that long, they can't be THAT bad, right?

-Mr. Kipper

FURTHER INVESTIGATIONS

CASE #FTM09SAP

1. In this book, the whole sixth grade (including me) went on a field trip. What field trips have you gone on? Which one was your favorite, and why?

2. What's the best part of visiting an amusement park?

3. Who else could have been a suspect in this mystery?

IN YOUR OWN DETECTIVE'S NOTEBOOK . . .

1. Design your own amusement park. What kinds of rides does it have? What about food? Don't forget to give it a name!

2. Gum, Egg, Cat, and I are best friends. Write about your best friend. Don't forget to include what you like about your friend.

3. This book is a mystery story. Write your own mystery story!